# Dear Parent:
## Your child's love of reading starts here!

Every child learns to read in a different way and at his or her own speed. Some go back and forth between reading levels and read favorite books again and again. Others read through each level in order. You can help your young reader improve and become more confident by encouraging his or her own interests and abilities. From books your child reads with you to the first books he or she reads alone, there are I Can Read Books for every stage of reading:

### SHARED READING
Basic language, word repetition, and whimsical illustrations, ideal for sharing with your emergent reader

### BEGINNING READING
Short sentences, familiar words, and simple concepts for children eager to read on their own

### READING WITH HELP
Engaging stories, longer sentences, and language play for developing readers

### READING ALONE
Complex plots, challenging vocabulary, and high-interest topics for the independent reader

### ADVANCED READING
Short paragraphs, chapters, and exciting themes for the perfect bridge to chapter books

I Can Read Books have introduced children to the joy of reading since 1957. Featuring award-winning authors and illustrators and a fabulous cast of beloved characters, I Can Read Books set the standard for beginning readers.

A lifetime of discovery begins with the magical words "I Can Read!"

*Visit www.icanread.com for information on enriching your child's reading experience.*

I Can Read Book® is a trademark of HarperCollins Publishers.

Berenstain Bears: We Love Soccer! Copyright © 2016 by Berenstain Publishing, Inc. All rights reserved. Manufactured in U.S.A. No part of this book may be used or reproduced in any manner whatsoever without written permission except in the case of brief quotations embodied in critical articles and reviews. For information address HarperCollins Children's Books, a division of HarperCollins Publishers, 195 Broadway, New York, NY 10007.
www.icanread.com

Library of Congress Control Number: 2015943562
ISBN 978-0-06-235014-5 (trade bdg.) — ISBN 978-0-06-235013-8 (pbk.)

16  17  18  19   LSCC   10 9 8 7 6 5 4 3     ❖     First Edition

# The Berenstain Bears®

# WE LOVE SOCCER!

## Mike Berenstain

Based on the characters created by
Stan and Jan Berenstain

**HARPER**

*An Imprint of HarperCollinsPublishers*

Brother and Sister Bear love soccer.

They are good at it, too.

They can pass and dribble.

They can head the ball.

They can do corner kicks.

They are good at throw-ins.

They are good goalies.

Brother and Sister are on the Rockets.
They play other teams around Bear
Country.

The whole family goes to every game.

They cheer for Brother and Sister.

Papa and Honey are good at cheering.

But Mama does much more.

She drives Brother and Sister to practice.

She makes snacks for the team.

She raises money for new uniforms.

She is a good soccer mom.

But sometimes,

Mama is *too* good a soccer mom.

She cheers too loudly.

She jumps up and down.

She whistles.

She waves signs.

She blows horns.

It is too much.

Mama wants the cubs to play harder.

She thinks they should win every game.

She signs them up for games far away.

Brother and Sister don't like it.

They don't like it one bit.

Now it is time for soccer practice.

Mama calls Brother and Sister.

They don't answer.

She looks for them.

She can't find them.

Where are they?

They will miss practice!

Mama looks for the cubs.

They are not at the playground.

They are not at the park.

They are not down by
the swimming hole.
Where are they?

Mama hears cubs laughing
and shouting.
It is coming from behind a
big sign.
There is an empty field
behind the sign.
Mama peeks around the sign.

Mama sees Brother and Sister
playing soccer.

They do not have uniforms.

They do not have real goals.

There are no coaches or refs.

There are no grown-ups at all.

There are just cubs having fun.

Hmm! Mama says to herself.

She is a good soccer mom.

But maybe she forgot something.

Maybe she forgot to let the cubs just have fun.

And having fun is what playing a game is all about.

Mama steps onto the field.

"Hey!" she calls. "Over here!

Pass the ball!"

"Look!" says Sister. "It's Mama!"

"I guess she wants to play," says Brother.

He kicks the ball to Mama.

She kicks the ball—hard!

The ball sails into the goal.

"Great kick!" the cubs yell. "Yay, Mama!"

"Hey, Mama!" says Sister.

"You're good!"

"You bet," says Mama.

"Let's play soccer!"

Papa and Honey cannot find Mama.

They cannot find Brother and Sister.

They go looking for them.

They meet grown-ups from the

soccer team.

They are also looking for their cubs.

They find them playing in the field.

"Hmm!" says Papa. "That looks fun!"

Papa and Honey join the game.

The other grown-ups join in, too.

They have a lot of fun!

It is getting dark.

The game ends.

Everyone goes home.

They are tired but happy.

"Could you teach us how to play better?" asks Sister.

"You bet," says Mama. "That would be fun!"

And having fun is what playing a game is all about.